Copyright © 2015 Disney Enterprises, Inc.

Published by Hallmark Gift Books,
a division of Hallmark Cards, Inc.,
Kansas City, MO 64141
Visit us on the Web at Hallmark.com.

Editorial Director: Carrie Bolin
Editor: Alyssa Kimmel
Art Director: Chris Opheim
Designer: Dan Horton

ISBN: 978-1-59530-817-7
BOK2220
Printed and bound in China

MAY15

Adapted by Bill Scollon and Alyssa Kimmel
Based on the episode written by Thomas Hart
Illustrated by Loter, Inc.

When Mickey and his friends get together, they always find an adventure!
Today, Mickey and his pals are pretending to be superheroes.

"Superheroes work together to save the day from super-villains," Mickey explains.

Donald pretends to be the bad guy. "You'll never defeat me," he shouts.

The superheroes join the fun and chase Donald every which way.
"Wait! We're supposed to work as a super-team," Mickey says,
but the heroes don't listen and end up in a jumble!
Just then, a shadow falls over the gang.

"Gawrsh!" says Goofy. "It's a giant hot dog balloon."

"That's a zeppelin," says Mickey. "But what is it doing here?"

Suddenly, Power-Pants Pete flies down. "Stay back," he warns.

"I'm about to shrink everything!"

Power-Pants Pete flies off, leaving the gang very worried.

"We have to stop Pete from shrinking everything!" says Mickey.

Goofy scratches his head. "This is a super-problem," he says.

"Did someone say 'super?'" a voice asks. It was Professor Von Drake!

"I have just the thingamajig you need!"

The professor has a new invention. "I call it the Super-Maker Machine," he says.

"It makes soup?" asks Goofy.

"No, Goofy," laughs the professor. "It will make real superheroes out of all of you."

"Super cheers," says Mickey. "That's just what we need!"

"Then step right in," the professor says.

One by one, each of the gang is transformed into a superhero!
"Now you'll have super fantastic powers," the professor exclaims,
"but you'll have to work together to stop Power-Pants Pete."
"Don't worry," says Mickey. "The Super Heroes are on the job!"

"One more thing," the professor adds. "You'll only have your powers for a little while. When your Superpower Bands turn red, your powers will go kaput."

"Then we'd better get going!" says Minnie.

As the heroes hurry to find Power-Pants Pete, Goofy and
Donald get twisted and don't even notice the zeppelin floating
above them. Suddenly, Pete falls out and lands with a THUD!
"You're through, Power-Pants Pete!" says Super Mickey.
"I'm sorry," says Pete, "but the big boss made me do it!"

The zeppelin lands and out comes the big boss—Megamort! "It's shrinking time," he says. Megamort makes Pete tiny with his shrink ray.

"Megamort!" says Minnie. "You're just a mean ol' meany villain."

"And you haven't seen the last of me!" he says as he jumps in the zeppelin and takes off again.

Back on the ground, Tiny Pete is rolling down a hill! The heroes try to catch him, but they trip over each other and fall into a heap.

"Tiny Pete is rolling away and our Superpower Bands are turning red!" says Daisy. Because they aren't working together, the Super Heroes lose all their superpowers.

Up in the zeppelin, Megamort starts shrinking everything he sees! Mickey tries to stop him, but without any superpowers, it's no good. He is shrunk!

Tiny Mickey tells Pluto to go find the Super Heroes, but before any help can arrive, Megamort scoops up Mickey and takes him to the zeppelin.

Minnie and the rest of the heroes are still trying to save Tiny Pete, but Pete hits a bump and is launched in the air!

Minnie, Donald, and Daisy chase him down, and Goofy uses his long arms to reach out and make the catch! "We did it," says Minnie. "We worked together as a team."

All at once, the gang is turned back into superheroes! "When we work together," says Minnie, "we're super-duper!" Minnie looks up. "Uh oh. Megamort has captured Mickey!"

"We gotta save him," says Goofy.

The heroes hop in their super-jet to chase after the zeppelin, but the zeppelin springs a leak and flies out of control.

"Megamort needs help!" shouts Minnie.

"But he's a villain," says Goofy.

"He still needs saving," says Minnie, "and that's what Super Heroes do!"

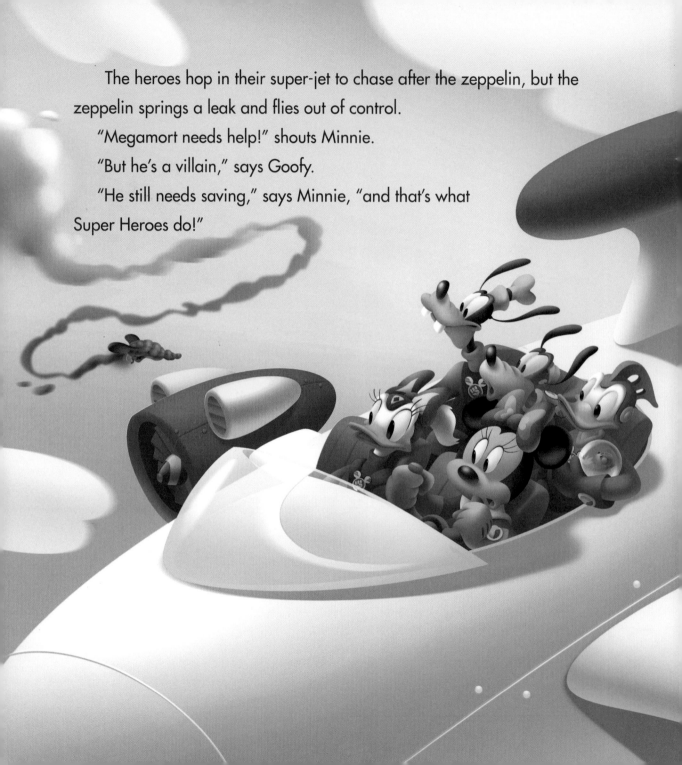

Pluto helps Minnie tie up the zeppelin. Then Donald and Goofy grab the ribbons and pull. Soon, the rest of the gang joins them. Everyone works together to pull the zeppelin to the ground.

"We did it!" they shout.

Megamort scrambles out of the flattened zeppelin. "After all I did, I can't believe you rescued me," he says. "Thank you."

Megamort reverses the shrink ray and returns Mickey and Pete to their normal sizes.

"I'm sorry," Megamort says. "Sometimes I don't know how to be a friend, because I don't have any."

"Well, you do now!" says Goofy.

"That's super!" Megamort says.

"It's more than super," says Mickey. "It's super-duper!"

Did you enjoy this book?
We'd love to hear from you.

Please send your comments to:
Hallmark Book Feedback
P.O. Box 419034
Mail Drop 100
Kansas City, MO 64141

Or e-mail us at:
booknotes@hallmark.com